BeastQuest
NEW BLOOD
ADAM BLADE

With special thanks to Allan Frewin Jones

For Luke Rogerson, a great reader of books.

ORCHARD BOOKS

First published in Great Britain in 2020 by The Watts Publishing Group

1 3 5 7 9 10 8 6 4 2

Text © 2020 Beast Quest Limited
Cover illustrations by KJA Artists © Beast Quest Limited 2020
Inside illustrations by Dynamo © Beast Quest Limited 2020

Beast Quest is a registered trademark of Beast Quest Limited
Series created by Beast Quest Limited, London

A CIP catalogue record for this book is available from the British Library.

ISBN 978 1 40836 141 2

Printed in Great Britain

MIX
Paper from
responsible sources
FSC® C104740

The paper and board used in this book are made from wood from responsible sources

Orchard Books
An imprint of Hachette Children's Group
Part of The Watts Publishing Group Limited
Carmelite House, 50 Victoria Embankment, London EC4Y 0DZ

An Hachette UK Company
www.hachette.co.uk
www.hachettechildrens.co.uk

THE
LOST TOMB

ORCHARD

MEET THE GUARDIANS

SAM

BEAST POWER: Fire
LIKES: The beach
DISLIKES: Being told what to do

AMY

BEAST POWER: Storm
LIKES: Sports
DISLIKES: Injustice

CHARLIE

BEAST POWER: Water
LIKES: Puzzles
DISLIKES: Heights

PROLOGUE

"Malvel's mistake was believing he could conquer Earth with magic." Illia Raven picked up a fragment of rainbow-coloured eggshell with a pair of tweezers. "He should have paid more attention to technology. He should have paid more attention to *me*!"

She was alone in her laboratory, speaking her thoughts out loud to her robotic assistant. She rested the piece of shell in a meshwork cradle on her workbench. Cables ran to a series of complex electronic devices. Dials flicked as the instruments detected the shell's faint energy signal.

It was a piece of the shell from which the creature they called Wuko had hatched – the Beast that belonged to that deaf girl. She and the other two so-called Guardians were a problem that needed to be dealt with ... quickly and harshly, if Illia Raven's plans were to be fulfilled.

"The next encounter won't end so well for you children," she vowed under her breath. She recalled the battle on Malvel's yacht. After his defeat, she'd had to make a quick getaway to survive. It was frustrating to be beaten by three weakling kids. Embarrassing, too. "Guardians, are you? When I'm finished, you won't be fit to guard against household germs!"

She turned to the robot, a slender, elegant creation of shining chrome with long spindly arms, and clamps and pincers for fingers.

She glanced at the robot's blank silver face, not caring that it didn't understand a word she said. "Magic and technology combined – that's the answer."

Her fingers danced over the keyboard of her laptop. A series of complex equations came and went. Green lines zigzagged across charts. Pulses of energy rose and fell.

A triumphant grin spread across her face. "I was right! Guardians and their eggs are linked by a unique energy frequency. That's why only Guardians can hatch eggs, and that's how they bond with their Beasts."

She tapped out a series of commands on her laptop. The image of a metallic headband appeared on the screen.

"My beautiful energy crown," she murmured, her eyes shining. "It's time for you to become reality." She pressed a key and a 3-D printer whirred into action.

"Soon, I'll have the powers of a

Guardian." She could barely contain her excitement. "I'll be able to hatch a Beast egg – and control whatever creature is born from it. All I need is an unhatched Beast egg."

She strode across the laboratory to a roof-vent near where a circular drone with four jet engines stood. Connected by clamps to the underside of the hoop was a large ball of segmented grey metal.

Illia fingered a control device on her wrist. The jets growled and the vent slid open, revealing a square of blue sky.

She entered more commands and the drone rose from the floor, humming as its motors gained power.

"Go and fetch me that unhatched Beast egg, my lovely," Illia crooned as the drone lifted through the vent. "Make me proud."

ONE

"London is totally awesome," Sam sighed, raindrops dripping off the peak of his baseball cap. "But your climate is strictly for ducks!"

Amy laughed at her Californian cousin. "This is the first rain in weeks," she reminded him.

Amy, Sam and Charlie were walking beside the lake known as the Serpentine, in Hyde Park. Across the rain-stippled water, blue pedal boats were moored along the quay, and ahead of them the Serpentine Bar with its pagoda-like white roof was all but deserted.

"If we were in L.A., I could take you guys to surf Zuma Beach," Sam continued. He posed, leaning forward, knees bent, arms outstretched for balance. "Have you ever tried surfing?"

"Once, when I was visiting my mum's folks in China," Amy said. "A place called Hainan Island. There were some big waves."

That was the first time she'd tried her waterproof hearing processors. They were a little bulkier than the usual ones, but they'd worked fine. In fact, she was wearing them right now, in case a stray flurry of rain got in under her umbrella. As her mum always said, better safe than sorry.

"I've seen surfers in Brighton," Charlie chimed in. "Looked dangerous, though, and I couldn't work out how they kept their balance."

"Dude, you need more fun in your life," Sam said.

"Finding stuff out *is* my idea of fun," Charlie replied with a smile. "For instance, did you know that the highest wave ever surfed was 24.38 metres?"

Sam grinned. "Where do you store all this information?"

"In my head," Charlie said. "What do you keep in yours?"

"My head's a permanent party zone." Sam laughed. "And everyone's invited."

They had come to an avenue of tall trees. In the distance, Amy could see the Houses of Parliament. But what she was really looking for was Wuko.

She spotted him, swinging from branch to branch, a small hyperactive bundle of fur, whooping and chattering to himself while Sam's little dragon, Spark, zipped between the trunks like a guided missile.

The rainy summer's day had its benefits, Amy thought. It meant Spark and Wuko could get some exercise in the park without too much chance of freaking people out.

Her heart swelled at the sight of her Beast. "I've never loved anything like I love Wuko," she sighed.

"I'm pleased for you." Charlie sounded fed up. "Hope *my* egg hatches soon."

Amy gave him a sympathetic look. Charlie had been so excited to find that blue Beast egg in Brighton. He carried it everywhere with him, nestled safely in his backpack – but two whole weeks had gone by, and still it showed no signs of activity.

"It'll happen," Sam assured him. "Be patient."

Charlie frowned. "But your eggs hatched out almost straight away," he complained.

"Mine just sits there."

"Your Beast will come when it's good and ready," Amy reassured him.

She touched the Seeing Eye amulet under her shirt. When activated, it revealed the hiding place of every Beast egg on the planet. Amy knew their Avantian friend and mentor, Karita, would soon need to seek out more of the eggs. But for the moment, now that the Dark Wizard Malvel had been banished, the three young Guardians were enjoying some much-needed downtime.

It's a pity Illia Raven escaped. In some ways, she was worse than Malvel. He wasn't from Earth, so at least he had some excuse for wreaking such havoc here ...

Amy's thoughts were interrupted by three sudden noises: Wuko giving a loud screech of fright; Spark letting out a piercing hiss; and Sam yelling, "*Incoming!*"

Amy whipped her umbrella out of the way to see what was happening. Something was plummeting out of the rain-filled sky. Four jet engines on a circular frame – and beneath it, a big ball of grey metal.

"It's a drone," Charlie cried. "And it's coming right at us!"

"Get it together, Guardians!" shouted Sam. "We know who sent this!" A moment later, the long metal chain snaked out of his Arcane Band, which he wore on his wrist. He whirled it around his head, the hook on the end of the chain humming in the wind. "Bring it on, Illia!" he called. "We're ready for you!"

Amy dropped her umbrella and focused on her own wristband. She felt a surge of power as her long, spiked mace grew in her hand. Beside her, Charlie's silvery axe glimmered in the light.

They were ready!

The clamps released and the metal ball thudded to the ground between the Guardians and the trees.

Spark and Wuko hurried closer while Amy and her cousins moved in from the other side. They stepped back in alarm as the ball unfolded to reveal a curved, armoured back, sturdy legs and a wedge-shaped head with flaring green eyes. A tail of thick steel bands thrashed dangerously.

"It's some kind of mechanical armadillo," Amy gasped. As she spoke, two hatches on the monster's back flipped open and twin blasters shot up. One fired a bolt of green fire at Sam, while the other pivoted around and blasted towards Wuko and Spark.

Sam hurled himself flat in the grass, the whip of green fire cutting into his shoulders as the two Beasts flung themselves aside to avoid the blast.

With a yell of anger, Charlie launched himself at the robot. He brought his axe down hard on the metal head, but the blade

bounced off and he was sent staggering back.

Amy moved in from the other side, enraged that the war-machine was firing at her beloved Wuko. She struck its blaster with all her strength. Her arms stung from the impact, but it had no effect. She was about to deliver a second blow when her feet were whipped out from under her by the thrashing tail.

Gasping from the fall, she scrambled away before the robot's metal feet could stomp her into the ground.

"Remain where you are, and no one need be hurt," a voice rang out from the machine.

A third hatch opened in the monster's back and a cone of light was projected into the air. Illia Raven stood in the beam, her red hair framing her sly, smirking face, her body clad in the familiar green leather.

A hologram!

"Listen up, kids," she said. "We can do this the easy way, or the hard way."

As she spoke, the armadillo's blaster kept Spark and Wuko at bay. The other weapon was trained on the cousins, but didn't fire.

"Keep talking," shouted Sam. "Since you're too cowardly to face us in person."

"Chill out, *dude*!" mocked Illia. "All I want is the egg you retrieved from Brighton. Hand it over and I promise, no harm will come to you." Her fingers moved to her chest. "Cross my heart!"

"That's never going to happen!" cried Charlie.

"And I thought you were the smart one," Illia teased. She raised her hand. "Keep your eyes on me, kids. I have a trick to show you."

Amy watched her suspiciously. *What is she up to?*

From the corner of her eye, Amy noticed a movement in the grass.

She's distracting us so we won't see what's really happening!

A slender metal tendril slid past her, thin as an adder, silent and swift.

It's coming from the mouth of the

mechanical armadillo!

"Charlie, watch out!" Amy shouted. The tip of the armadillo's tongue sprang up, looping around Charlie's backpack and wrenching it from his shoulders.

The tendril rose into the air, the backpack containing the precious egg dangling as Charlie leaped to snatch at it. His fingers missed by a fraction and he dropped down with a cry of anguish.

"Sam, help me!" Amy jumped up and raced across the grass. Sam rose, swinging his chain around his head, gathering speed. Amy leaped, grasping the chain and allowing it to boost her into the air.

At the perfect moment, she released her

grip and launched herself at the backpack. Her fingers closed on a strap. But even as she hung there, she saw the jet-studded hoop plunge to reattach itself to the armadillo.

The drone lifted into the sky and the armadillo's tongue reeled in.

"Amy!" Sam's anxious cry came up to her. She was already at tree-top height. If she hung on, she would be carried off by the drone – but if she fell, she could be badly injured, and the egg would be lost.

Clinging on, she felt the topmost branches of the trees brushing her feet.

There was nothing she could do.

TWO

Sam watched in horror as Amy was carried over the trees. He flung his chain upward, but the drone was already out of reach.

He could see branches swishing and waving wildly above him. *That must be Wuko, trying to get to Amy.* He turned to Spark. The little dragon was snorting steam and quivering with anger.

Sam projected his thoughts towards her.

Amy's in trouble. Help Wuko!

Spark gave a little roar and soared for the treetops just as Wuko's grimacing face appeared above the branches.

Spark hovered over him, letting out sharp cries.

The furry Beast grabbed Spark's legs as she rose, flapping her wings furiously as she struggled with the extra weight.

Charlie stood at Sam's side. "That's what I call teamwork," he said.

Spark drew closer to the drone and Wuko leaped, pressing his hand against one of the engines.

"He's sucking the energy out of it!" Charlie said.

The jet faltered, then died. The drone tipped and wheeled awkwardly as Wuko bounded to the second engine.

The drone began to lose height, circling erratically. It smashed through the trees and landed with a crash.

"Amy!" Sam and Charlie ran forwards.

She wasn't there.

The drone was broken and the armadillo lay on its back, its thick legs struggling. Bursts of green fire sprayed out from its blasters and its tail whipped back and forth.

With a yell, Amy dropped from the canopy of branches, bringing her mace down on the machine with all her strength. The mace dug deep, cracking open the metal hide, sending sparks flying. The lashes of green fire died away and the legs became still.

Suddenly, the armadillo's mouth sprang open and its long silvery tongue lashed out at Sam.

"Ow!" Sam clutched his arm, feeling a stab of pain.

Charlie severed the steel tongue with one swipe of his axe.

Amy gave the machine another whack with her mace. There was a sizzling noise then silence. "Are you hurt?" she asked Sam.

He rubbed his arm. "It's nothing." In fact, it stung really badly.

Wuko dropped from the tree on to Amy's shoulder. He nuzzled her face, chattering with pleasure. She stroked him. "Well done!"

Spark zipped in under the trees and landed on top of Sam's head. Sam took a treat out of his pocket and threw it into the air. The dragon breathed fire and caught the toasted morsel in her jaws. She sat on his head, chewing contentedly.

"Where's my bag?" Charlie asked, looking around. "Oh no!" The backpack had fallen into a hollow filled with rainwater.

He crouched beside the puddle. "It's come open," he groaned. "My egg's all wet."

"Your Guardian sigil is water," said Amy. "A bit of rain won't ... ohhh!" Her eyes widened as she leaned over Charlie and the egg.

Sam saw a crack run along the shell. "It's hatching!"

"It needed water," gasped Charlie. "I should have worked that out!"

The three cousins held their breath as the egg cracked open.

An extraordinary Beast emerged. The closest thing Sam thought it resembled was a large newt. It had slinky blue-green scales and a blunt, rounded head topped by two big, blinking eyes. Spines ran along its back and its tail swished from side to side as it clambered out of the broken shell. That was when Sam noticed it had

six legs that ended in little hands with wide-spread fingers.

"She's called Sali," Charlie said, without having to ask. He just *knew*. "She's ... *wonderful*!"

"I wonder what she does?" asked Amy, reaching out.

The Beast stared around herself then sprang into the air, almost bowling Charlie over.

As they watched in astonishment, the water Beast bounded and rebounded among the trees, zigzagging so quickly that they could hardly keep track of her.

"Lively little thing, isn't she?" gasped Sam as the Beast whipped past him.

Charlie scrambled to his feet and ran after her. "Don't be scared," he called.

The Beast dived into a rain-puddle.

And vanished.

"Wha-at?" Charlie stepped into the shallow water. "Where did she go?"

"There!" yelled Amy, pointing. The Beast burst from a different puddle, moving at high speed. She dived headlong into another pool and was gone again.

Charlie let out a yelp of surprise as Sali erupted out of the pool at his feet. He raced after her as she bounded across the grass, heading for the lake.

"Catch her, Charlie!" Amy shouted. "We should take her to Karita's castle – she'll know how to control her."

Charlie flung himself at the Beast and caught her in mid-air as she jumped out over the lake.

He turned to the others. "Phew!" he gasped. "That was lucky!"

The Beast squirmed frantically in his hands. Charlie staggered back, overbalanced and fell into the water.

Sam and Amy ran for the lake.

The water seethed and bubbled for a few moments. Ripples spread slowly.

Sam and Amy looked at one another, aghast.

Charlie and his new Beast were gone.

THREE

Barely had the water closed over Charlie's head before he was catapulted into the air again. He landed facedown on gravel.

He groaned at the impact, but his first thought was for his newly hatched Beast.

He lifted his head. Sali was squatting in the gravel about a metre away, staring at him with big blinking eyes. Beyond her, he saw walls of thick stone.

Uh-oh! We aren't in Hyde Park any more.

"Where have you taken us?" he gasped.

Feet crunched in the gravel. Black leather boots approached. Charlie saw a leather coat and a woman's face with fierce green eyes, framed by dark, purple-streaked hair. In one hand, the woman held a long whitewood pole. At her side paced a huge, magnificent panther.

"Karita!" Charlie breathed. "Varla!" Behind them, Karita's Avantian-style castle towered, topped with battlements and turrets.

"Where did you come from, Charlie?" Karita asked, helping him to his feet. Her eyes moved past him. "And what is that?"

Charlie turned. Behind him, water leaped

skywards from a round stone fountain. Before he could speak, two figures shot out of the fountain, surprise and alarm stamped on their faces. Sam and Amy both managed to land on their feet, Wuko clinging to Amy's neck and Spark perched on Sam's shoulder.

They're dry! Oh – and so am I. This is weird!

"Welcome, Guardians," said Karita, looking at Charlie's Beast. "I see the third egg has hatched."

"Sali needed to be in water to hatch," said Charlie.

"Remarkable. The Beast can open portals through water," Karita said. "A useful power, to be sure, but how did she know to bring you here?"

Charlie thought about it. "I had the image of your castle in my head when we fell into the lake," he said. "She must have picked up on it."

"And the portal stayed open long enough for us to follow," said Amy. "Cool!"

"I know of no other Beast with such abilities," said Karita, turning to Charlie. "All you need do is visualise a place, and if there is water nearby, she can take you there. An amazing power."

"She can help us get to all the other Beast eggs," said Sam, tapping Charlie on the shoulder. "That's genius."

"And I think we need to get moving on that," added Amy. She turned to Karita. "Illia Raven is back."

Rapidly, the three cousins filled Karita in on their encounter with Malvel's deadly accomplice.

"She wanted Charlie's egg," Amy said.

"Maybe she's found out how to hatch it," added Charlie.

Karita's eyes blazed. "That must never happen."

"But I thought Beasts were good?" Sam said.

"Beasts can be corrupted if they are hatched by a bad person," Karita explained. She looked intently at Amy. "Where is the

Seeing Eye amulet?"

"Right here." Amy drew it out.

"Activate it," Karita said. "Watch the images, Guardians – call out if you recognise anything."

Amy held the amulet up, the red jewel glowing. A beam of light sprayed out, filled with a rapid slideshow of images ...

A wall of skulls. A clock against a green background. The golden face of a woman. A serpent eating its own tail. A stone statue of a man with a dog's head.

"That's Anubis," Charlie cried, pointing. "The Egyptian god of the dead." He pulled out his mobile phone and scrolled through his saved images file. "Yes!" He held up the phone, showing the others a picture of the same statue. "I was researching Egyptian mythology for a school project. That statue is in Karnak. It's a complex of temples on the Nile, thousands of years old."

"Good!" Karita nodded. "Charlie, see if Sali can open a portal there."

"I'll try." Charlie turned to the little Beast. Varla had paced over to her and was sniffing her with interest. Sali blinked up at the shadow panther then her long thin tongue flicked out, licking the panther's muzzle.

"Sali? Listen ..." Charlie began. The Beast looked at him, then bounded into the air. She landed on the rim of the fountain.

"She's connected to you," said Amy. "Now think of the temples where we want to go."

Charlie ran over to the fountain; the others followed close behind. Sali was already staring into the water. An image formed among the ripples like a shimmering painting. Pillars of cream-coloured stone, etched with hieroglyphics, were set against a blue sky.

"Hieroglyphics!" said Sam. "It must be Karnak."

"Well done, Sali," said Charlie. "But we need to plan this out before we go. We'll want sunscreen and hats for the heat. Egyptian money. Some food and water. Passports."

Sam jumped up on to the edge of the fountain, Spark on his shoulder. "I've always wanted to see a Nile crocodile!"

Before anyone could react, and with Spark clinging to his shoulder, Sam jumped off the stone edge and vanished into the water.

FOUR

my stared into the portal where Sam had just vanished. She could tell Charlie wasn't amused by their cousin's sudden exit.

"Why does he always have to rush in without thinking?" Charlie said.

"Quick – we need to get after him!" exclaimed Amy. "We'll have to do without the sunscreen." She took Wuko in her arms and leaped into the fountain with Charlie right behind. She braced herself for the cold water.

Good thing I'm wearing my waterproof hearing processors!

But there was no wetness – just a rushing, tumbling darkness, until her instep caught on something hard, tipping her forwards. Wuko leaped clear as she fell on to her hands and knees.

She was in a brightly lit room with Charlie sprawled at her side, gasping for breath.

"This can't be Karnak," Amy said, scrambling to her feet as Wuko jumped back into her arms.

She glanced over her shoulder and saw a row of sinks under a long mirror. Water was pouring from one of the taps.

We came through a tap?

The room held a row of cubicles, and there were white porcelain fixtures on the walls.

"We're in a toilet!" gasped Charlie.

"Chill out, dude!" Sam stood by a sink nearby, speaking to an alarmed-looking man in shorts and a T-shirt. "It's just a really cool-looking robodrone, that's all." The man was staring at Spark, who sat on Sam's shoulder with steam rising from her nostrils.

When Amy approached, the man gaped at her. Wuko grinned and gave him a friendly wave.

With a shriek, the man fled from the room.

"I guess we freaked him out," said Sam.

"You think?" Charlie picked Sali up. "Why did you bring us to a public loo?"

"It could have been worse." Sam grinned. "We could have come up through one of the toilets."

"Only a boy would think of that!" said Amy in disgust. "That guy's T-shirt had an image of the Karnak temple complex on it. Maybe Sali got confused?"

"No way," Charlie said defensively. He looked down his Beast's big, goggling eyes. "You didn't, did you?" Sali squirmed out of his arms and leaped up on to the wall, frowning down at him as though outraged by his doubts.

"Sorry, guys," Charlie murmured. "Mistakes happen – and she's only just hatched."

"Let's find out where we are," said Sam. "Spark – undercover time." Spark slid into Sam's open backpack.

Charlie reached up and plucked Sali off the wall. The little Beast allowed herself to be pushed into the front of Charlie's shirt, but she squirmed around inside his clothes as if she didn't like being there. "Stay still, Sali!" Charlie said. "You can come out in a little while."

Sali quietened down, but Amy got the

impression Charlie and his Beast weren't getting on too well.

They made their way into a very modern room of polished sand-coloured stone with stairways and balconies and soaring walls. Displayed around the room were brown-stone statues, carved heads and other ancient artefacts.

People were wandering about examining the exhibits, some in Arabic dress, others in T-shirts and shorts.

"We're in Luxor Museum," exclaimed Charlie. "I did a virtual tour of this place online for that school project I was telling you about." He indicated a statue in a timeworn Egyptian headdress. "That's

King Thutmose the Third."

Amy got out her phone and did a quick map search.

"We're only one and a half kilometres from Karnak," she said to Charlie. "Sali was pretty close."

"Good girl, Sali," said Charlie, gently patting the bulge in his shirt-front before taking out his own phone. "There must be an floor plan of the temple complex online. I'll check it out while we walk there."

When they exited the museum, they stepped into fierce sunlight and blistering heat. Amy could hardly catch her breath in the scorching air. Tall palm trees hung over brown brick walkways and green lawns.

Imposing statues of gods and pharaohs stared down from tall plinths.

Ahead of them, the Nile slid past, sparkling sapphire blue. On the far bank, palm trees waved among square brown buildings. Boats glided along, their white sails like resting butterflies.

"What an amazing place," breathed Amy, captivated by the glorious view. "I can't believe I'm in Egypt."

And it only took us a second to get here!

She consulted her phone. "This way," she said, pointing to the right.

They walked along the riverbank, slowly getting used to the heat, chatting excitedly about the wonders they were seeing.

The wide road shimmered in the heat as cars whizzed past plodding donkey carts. Stately palms soared on long slender trunks, bare save for a burst of green fronds at the top. Modern white buildings glowed among time-eaten stone walls, their windows shining like silver.

Amy breathed in the scent of exotic spices, her implants picking up the calls of street vendors wearing skullcaps and loose-fitting ankle-length robes. She saw young women in hijabs and with colourful tunics over blue jeans, taking selfies among ancient sandstone ruins.

It's such an amazing mix of old and new.

"Guys," said Sam. "Feast your eyes on that!"

Amy breathed out a gasp at the sight. Ahead of them, the temple ruins showed stark against the sky – stone walls and massive pillars stretched back from the river, cracked and crumbling with age, but still echoing the power and might of ancient Egypt.

"Awesome!" breathed Sam.

Amy agreed. It really was awesome.

And that feeling only grew as they approached the vast complex.

"Are there mummies?" asked Sam.

"This isn't a tomb," Charlie said, scrolling through the website he'd found. "But there's an enormous necropolis on the other side of the river."

"A *what*-opolis?" asked Sam.

"It's a huge cemetery," Charlie explained. "Three and a half thousand years old."

"Full of mummies?" Sam asked eagerly.

"I suppose so," said Charlie.

"Cool!"

Amy shuddered – she'd seen too many horror movies about mummies to feel comfortable with that idea.

As she eyed the long line of people at the museum entrance, a disturbing thought hit her. "Uh, how do we pay the entrance fee?"

"See, this is what happens when you don't make plans," Charlie groaned, giving Sam a look. "We have no money, no sunscreen, no food, nothing!"

"Chill, bro," said Sam. "Maybe we can slip by unnoticed?"

"See those men?" Charlie said, pointing to armed guards standing by the entrance. "I think they'd have something to say if we tried to sneak in."

Amy's spirits sank.

We're so close – but how do we get in there to find the egg?

FIVE

Two choices, Sam thought, eyeing a low fence that encircled the temple complex. *Try to talk the others into it, or just go for it ...*

No contest!

He'd worked out a few commands for Spark – instructions for dangerous situations.

"Let's give them some fireworks, girl," he told the little dragon.

An instant later, Spark shot out of his backpack and soared into the air, flying far above the line of people waiting to enter the temple complex. At the apex of her flight, she spun around, releasing a roar of flame.

All eyes swivelled upwards. There was pointing and shouting.

"Let's go," Sam hissed to his cousins. Before they could reply, he sprinted to the fence and climbed over it.

A few seconds later, Charlie and Amy followed him over the fence.

"It's called a diversion," Sam explained as they stared at him in disbelief.

"You're out of your mind," gasped Amy.

Grinning, Sam made for a gap between the temple walls. His cousins raced after him until all three were safely inside and away from the guards along the perimeter.

"This is so wrong! Breaking into an ancient historical site!" Charlie gasped. "Sali could have taken us back to Karita's castle to get money for the entrance fee."

Sam rolled his eyes. "You think Karita has a lot of *Egyptian* money lying around?"

"We'll pay online when we get home," Amy told Charlie.

Spark streaked out of the sky and landed on Sam's shoulder. "Clever girl!" he said as the dragon slipped into his backpack. He turned to Charlie. "So how do we find the egg?"

"How am I supposed to know?" exclaimed Charlie. "You didn't give me time for any research."

"We look for the statue that the Seeing Eye showed us," Amy said calmly.

They walked past towering walls and came into a grand courtyard lined with massive ram-headed sphinxes. There were tourists wandering around, but no one took any notice of the cousins.

"Stunning," breathed Amy as they walked towards high sandstone walls, gnawed by the centuries but still magnificent. She held Wuko under her arm, immobile as a stuffed toy, but staring around with huge eyes. Sam grinned at the sight. Hopefully, anyone who noticed him would think Wuko was just a seriously weird-looking teddy bear.

Sali was having more trouble keeping out of sight. The Beast kept poking her head out of Charlie's shirt. "Sali, stay down," he urged, hurrying through a tall stone doorway. He gave a gasp. "This is the Great Temple of Amun," he said, gazing up at the colossal statues that lined the walls as the others followed him into the building.

Sam stared up at the solemn faces, shivers running down his spine. They had stood there for thousands of years, cracked and broken and eaten away by time, but overwhelming all the same, and just a bit scary. "Awesome!" he breathed. "Super-awesome!"

They moved from room to room, feeling the weight of years pressing in all around them.

Using the floor plan he'd found on his phone, Charlie guided them through a series of small rooms, each displaying amazing artefacts – hieroglyphs, statues and walls carved with scenes from Egyptian mythology.

"Found it!" Charlie exclaimed suddenly. "Anubis!"

They were alone in a small antechamber. A black statue of a man with a dog's head stared past them. Sam looked into the stern eyes.

"Look at this!" breathed Amy, crouching

beside the statue. There was a cracked fragment of stone lying against the plinth it stood on. The stone was carved with the sigils of Water, Fire and Storm – the symbols of each of their Guardian bloodlines.

As Amy leaned closer, her sigil – the sign of Storm – began to glow.

"It must be reacting to your Arcane Band," said Charlie, holding his arm above the stone. Instantly, the Water sigil came alive. Sam reached out, his Arcane Band tingling as the Fire sigil ignited.

There was a *clunk* from behind the statue. A block of stone swung away, revealing a low, dark slot in the wall.

Sam glanced around to make sure they were alone. "I guess we go in."

"First, I'll call Karita for an update," Amy said, pressing speed-dial. "In case we lose signal wherever we're going."

As Sam peered into the hole, Spark crawled from his backpack and sat on his shoulder with her tail wrapped loosely around his neck.

Karita answered immediately and Amy quickly filled her in on their progress, pausing to listen to her replies.

"Karita says Illia Raven isn't in England," Amy explained after the call ended. "Now Malvel's gone, she's the acting CEO of Obsidian Corp – and she's jetted off to the company's research lab in Dubai."

"That's only a few hours from here by plane," Charlie said anxiously.

"Relax, man," said Sam. "She doesn't know we're here." He activated the torch on his phone and crawled into the hole. "I hope it's bigger further in," he said.

His phone light showed a long crawl-space moving gradually downwards. The air was stale and dusty. The passage opened up after a while and the cousins found themselves at the head of a set of stone steps that plunged down into darkness.

"Whatever's down here is going to be older than anything above ground, and that means it's probably far less safe," warned Charlie as Sam began to descend. "We need to be really careful."

"OK, *Mom*," grinned Sam as he headed deeper. "Wow! I bet no one's seen any of this for thousands of years." His voice began to echo in an eerie way.

"If there's a Beast egg, some of our grandparents must have been here," Amy reminded him. "And don't forget the guards that protected the other eggs – we should prepare for trouble."

"That's a problem," said Charlie. "We could face Ancient Egyptian booby traps and Avantian booby traps combined." Sali squirmed under his shirt, as though she didn't like the idea, either.

"We're Guardians," said Sam confidently. "We'll deal with it."

The stairs ended and a narrow corridor led them to a chamber. As Sam stepped over the threshold, torches burst into flames all along the walls, filling the square room with dancing light.

"Wow!" gasped Sam, staring around. Every centimetre of the walls was covered in intricate hieroglyphs. A huge stone door filled most of the far wall, guarded on either side by statues of towering soldiers. Between them and the door lay a moat of clear water, barring their way forward.

Charlie peered into the water. "It's

deep," he said. "And there are stones at the bottom. Looks like they're carved like feathers." He looked at the others. "This water must come from the Nile – otherwise, it would have dried out centuries ago."

Sam stared at the colossal door. "We could swim across, I guess," he said. "But then what?"

"There's no door handle," added Amy. "How do we get it open?"

Charlie looked thoughtfully at the statues. "That one is Anput," he said, pointing to the statue on the left. "She's the female version of the god of death." He turned to the other statue. "And that's Anubis again – holding his scales."

Sam saw that the statue's raised hand held a set of old-fashioned weighing scales.

"The Egyptians believed that when a person died, Anubis weighed their hearts against a feather," said Charlie. "If the heart was too heavy, then the dead person would be eaten by a goddess that was part lion, part crocodile and part hippo. And if the heart was lighter, they'd be allowed into the afterlife."

"So, this is the door to the *afterlife*?" asked Amy. "Let's hope not."

"It must be a really old tomb," said Charlie, looking around excitedly.

"With a mummy?" asked Sam. "That would be great."

Charlie frowned at the statue of Anubis. "Maybe the door will open if we balance the scales so the side with the heart is lighter ..."

Sam noticed that the side of the scale where the feather should be was empty, and that the bowl holding a stone sculpture of a heart hung lower.

"Remember those feathers you saw in the water, Charlie?" said Amy. "Maybe one of them will outweigh the heart and open the door."

"Why bother with a feather?" Sam said. "Weighing it down with anything should work.

He picked up a chunk of cracked

sandstone that lay on the floor. "Spark – fly this over to the scales."

Spark took the rock in her claws and glided across the moat to the statue. She released the stone and it plopped into the bowl.

With a soft grating sound, the scales began to tilt.

"This is too easy!" grinned Sam. "The door is totally going to open now, and—"

The scales shuddered and a gush of flame launched the rock out of the bowl as the statue's long, dog-like jaw dropped open. A hot red light grew in the deep, dark throat.

"Uh-oh!"

A ball of fire burst out between the statue's teeth, striking Sam in the chest and throwing him backwards across the room.

SIX

"**S**am!" Amy screamed as her cousin was dashed against the far wall of the chamber. Flames licked around him as he sprawled on the floor. Spark darted towards the statue, breathing fire.

"I'm OK," gasped Sam, staggering to his feet. He looked dazed by the fall, and his shirt was partly scorched away at his chest and sleeve – but there were no burns on his skin, and already he had his hook and chain in his hand.

"Fire can't hurt me," Sam shouted at the statue. "What else have you got?"

A low, menacing hum sounded. Amy looked cautiously around. She could feel Wuko trembling, and his eyes were huge with alarm. "That rock didn't work. We must have to use the feathers," she said.

"And we've set off a trap," Charlie said.

The hum turned to a high-pitched screaming. Amy instinctively changed the setting on her implants to lessen the noise. She saw Sam and Charlie throw their hands over their ears, grimacing in pain at the ear-splitting shrieking.

The eyes of the wall-carvings began to

glow. A moment later, flames burst from every carved eye in the room, all of them aimed right at the three cousins.

Almost quicker than thought, Amy activated her Arcane Band, throwing up a shield that deflected the spears of fire. The shrieking faded to a roar.

At least the others won't be hampered by the noise now!

"Stand together!" Charlie yelled, jets of fire glancing off his own shield. "Back to back!"

They darted into the middle of the room, crouching, holding up their shields to ward off the torrent of fire.

Spark circled the chamber at high speed,

scorching the walls with her own blasts of fire. A few fireballs struck her, but the flames rolled harmlessly off her scales.

"This is no good," gasped Charlie, using his shield to protect Sam and Amy. "We have to get out of here."

"No, we need to open that door!" Sam shouted over the roar of the fireballs. "We can't back off now."

"We need to try one of those feathers from down in the water!" cried Amy, her arm aching from the deluge of flame that hammered against her shield. "That's what we need to balance the scales." Wuko was growling on her shoulder, eager to get out and fight the fireballs.

"No, Wuko!" Amy warned. "Stay here – you'll be burned!"

"Move together," said Sam. "Towards the moat."

Keeping their shields up, they edged across the room. Kneeling at the brink of the moat, Sam reached down and plunged his arm into the water.

"It's too deep to reach the feathers!" he gasped. "I'm going in."

Amy caught him by the arm just as he was about to dive.

"Let Charlie try," she cried. "His bloodline is Water."

Charlie shot her an anxious look. "But how long will I have to hold my breath?"

"You've got Sali now," Amy reminded him. "She'll help."

Charlie touched the bulge in his shirt-front. Sali's head appeared, her big eyes staring into his. After a moment, astonishment filled Charlie's face.

"I heard her voice in my head!" he gasped. "She said she can help me hold my breath underwater. I'm going for it." His shield vanished back into his Arcane Band and he slid over the edge of the moat and plunged into the water.

Sam and Amy crouched back to back, fending off the storm of fire. Amy knew Sam didn't need to hide from the flames, but she was vulnerable, and his shield was

protecting her.

But her own shield was becoming uncomfortably hot, and tongues of flame licked greedily around the rim.

Could even Guardian shields survive this onslaught for long?

As though sensing her fears, Wuko leaped from Amy's shoulder and bounded across the floor, dodging fireballs.

"Wuko, no!" Amy was terrified that her Beast would be incinerated, but Wuko reached the wall unharmed. He pressed his hands to the stone. In a spreading circle around his splayed fingers, the eyes dimmed, and the flames went out.

He's draining the energy out of them!

Spark was also doing her part – scorching the walls and breathing soot into the blazing eyes of the attacking figures.

The rain of flame lessened as the two Beasts worked: Spark flying, Wuko leaping around the walls, his hands slapping the stone and dousing the flames.

Amy and Sam got to their feet. The torrent of fire had ended. Spark let out a triumphant shriek as Wuko bounced back to Amy, whooping in delight.

There was a soft splash at their backs.

"Got the heaviest one!" Charlie was treading water, holding a stone feather in his hand. "It was amazing! I could breathe underwater."

"Take it, Spark!" called Sam. "Put it on the scales." The dragon swooped down and clutched the feather in her claws.

She flew up to the empty scale and dropped the feather.

The scales shifted scratchily. There was a *click* as the heart rose just above the feather. With the rasp of stone on stone, the great door swung down across the moat, creating a pathway into another chamber beyond.

"Brilliant!" Charlie yelled, swimming towards his cousins.

A new sound filled the chamber. A rushing, sucking, gurgling noise.

With shocking speed, the water level

dropped, pulling Charlie down with it.

"Whoa!" he cried.

Amy sprang forward, falling to her knees and reaching out for Charlie's grasping fingers. "Grab my hand!" she cried.

Terror distorted Charlie's face as his fingertips brushed Amy's for a moment before he was swept away from her. The water swirled and churned as it drained.

Sali clung with all six of her feet to Charlie's shirt-front.

He gave a final despairing look. "Guys! I—"

The water raced away through a gaping slot in the bottom of the moat.

Charlie and Sali were gone.

SEVEN

When the world stopped spinning around him, Charlie realised he was still underwater. He held his breath, the air ringing in his ears, his chest tightening in pain. He needed to breathe.

Far, far above him, he saw quivering lights.

Deep water. Not good.

Something crawled up his chest. He looked down and saw Sali blinking up at him, her six feet clinging to his shirt.

As he stared into her eyes, the pain in his chest faded away. He didn't need to breathe any more. It was like Sali was giving him air with her touch.

Her eyes swivelled, looking up beyond him.

He began to swim upward with Sali still clutching at his chest.

His head broke the surface and he gulped in air. The lights he had seen were flaming torches fixed to the walls of a large flooded chamber. The walls were massive stone blocks; the ceiling so high that it was lost in shadows.

Where am I?

In the centre of the chamber, a great slab of stone rose above the water. Sali let go of his shirt and began to swim rapidly towards it, her tail wriggling as she powered away.

Charlie followed, heaving himself on to the island and gazing up in amazement at a towering statue of a woman in a high, plumed headdress.

"I know who you are," Charlie said, getting to his feet. "You're Anuket, goddess of the Nile." He realised he was dry from head to foot.

Having a Water bloodline certainly saves a lot of squelching around in soggy clothes.

"I'm guessing this water comes from the

Nile," he said aloud. "Interesting."

Sali was sitting on the goddess's foot, watching him.

"Here's our problem," Charlie said, squatting beside his Beast. "Sam and Amy can't follow us now because all the water drained away. And we can't get back to them for the same reason – there's no water left up there for us to portal through. If I think of the fountain in Karita's castle, I'm sure you could take us there – but there's no way I'm leaving Amy and Sam stranded. So, we need a plan."

Sali blinked at him, her tail swishing slowly to and fro.

"No ideas, huh?" Charlie said. "Me

neither." He stood up and walked thoughtfully around the statue, hoping for inspiration. On the right heel, he saw a small circular projection – like a large stone button.

Hmmm.

He pressed down on it. A deep grinding noise reverberated around the chamber. Beside the far wall, he saw the water start to churn.

"It's some kind of underwater doorway," he said. "Sali – this is our way out!"

The Beast came scuttling around the statue and sprang into the water with a soft plop.

Charlie released the stone button,

intending to jump in after her. But after a moment, the grinding noise echoed again, and the churn of escaping water ceased.

He frowned. *Interesting.* He pressed his foot down on the button.

Griiiinnnddd. Chuuuurn.

He stepped away.

The door scraped shut again. The water became still.

"I see ..." Charlie said. "Well, that's annoying."

Sali swam back and crawled on to the plinth, looking questioningly at him.

"I'm thinking," he told her. He took off a shoe and rested it on the button.

Nothing happened.

"Not heavy enough." He removed his other shoe and his backpack, but he couldn't get everything to balance on the button. Discouraged, he put his shoes back on. "There's no way I can swim over there before the door closes." He stared across the chamber. "Even if you can portal us right to the door, it'll take too long."

His head drooped and Illia Raven's taunt echoed in his head. *I thought you were the smart one.*

Fear knotted his stomach and he let out a low groan.

"I don't know how to get us out of here, Sali," he said miserably.

He felt something touch his knee. Sali

was standing up on her back legs, looking into his eyes. Her mouth opened and her long slender tongue flicked out and licked his cheek.

She bounced on to his chest, all six feet kneading him, her tongue lapping his face.

He stroked the silky scales on her back, his fingers ticking across the smooth needles that ran along her spine.

"I wasn't sure if you liked me," he murmured.

Warm feelings came into his mind as Sali gently butted her blunt head against his chin. Then she bounded off and landed on the stone button.

Griinnd. Chuurrn.

Charlie jumped up. "That's genius," he gasped in delight. "I swim to the door while you hold it open. Then you portal over to me once I'm through."

Sali nodded her head.

"We're quite a team," Charlie said, walking to the edge of the plinth. He dived in, fearless of the water now that he had Sali to help him.

He let the suction of the water pull him through the hidden door.

"Sali! Quick!" he called.

He saw her leap and plunge into the water.

Griiinnnddd.

The little Beast appeared right in front of

him. He caught hold of her just as a *boom* sounded from the door closing behind them.

Now to find Sam and Amy!

EIGHT

"Oh, no, Charlie!" Sam shouted as the last of the water coursed away. "Quick!" he said to Amy. "We've got to follow them!" He leaped to the bottom of the moat and slipped in a puddle that was all that was left of the water that had rushed Charlie down into the dark slot where he'd vanished. Sam cried out and crashed on to his back.

Spark gave a shriek and flew to his side.

Amy jumped in after him. "Sam?"

"I'm OK," gasped Sam, biting back the pain. He heaved himself up. The slot in the bottom of the moat closed, like stone jaws clenching together.

Sam hacked at the thin line between the stones with the hook from his Arcane Band. "Open up!" But the hook didn't even make a scratch.

Spark sprayed the stones with fire, but the flames just boiled away, leaving no mark.

"Let Wuko try," said Amy. "He'll be full of the energy he drained from the wall carvings."

Sam backed off and Wuko swung down into the moat and pressed his hands against the crack. Fizzing white light exploded from his palms, sending shadows flying.

Still the stones didn't budge. Wuko looked regretfully at Amy as the white fire died from his hands.

"We have to get to Charlie!" Sam cried. "What's it going to take – dynamite?"

"He has Sali with him," Amy reassured him. "They're in water. They'll be able to portal out if he runs into any trouble."

Sam took a deep breath, working to calm himself. He was worried about Charlie. "So, what do *we* do?" he asked.

"We carry on," Amy said. "We're bound to meet up with them later." She sounded positive, but he could see the anxiety in her eyes.

Now that Wuko's energy beams had gone, the empty moat was full of shadows.

Amy let out a sudden cry. "Sam! What's with your *arm*?"

"Huh?" He twisted his arm around and saw that there was a tiny point of greenish light under the skin beneath his bicep. "What *is* that?"

"It's where you got hit by that armadillo-thing's tongue." Amy's eyes widened as she ran her finger over a little bump on Sam's skin. "There's something there."

"It must be a tracker," cried Sam, grasping his hook. "Illia Raven will have been following our movements the whole time. I've got to get it out."

He gritted his teeth, preparing to dig the hook into his flesh. But Wuko bounded on to his shoulder and flattened his hand over the small lump.

His big eyes glowed green for a moment, then he took his hand away.

The light from the tracker had gone out.

"He disabled it," said Amy. "Wuko – you're a marvel."

Wuko gave a whoop of joy and leaped to cling around Amy's neck.

"That's great," said Sam, rubbing his arm. "But it still means Illia knows where we are." A disturbing thought struck him. "Karita said she was in Dubai – but I bet she's on her way here."

"And at top speed!" added Amy. "We have to find Charlie, Sali and the egg before she arrives."

"Agreed," said Sam. He swung his hook up to catch the edge of the moat. They scrambled up the chain, ran across the bridge and raced through the gaping doorway. Wuko scampered alongside Amy while Spark flew over Sam's head.

As they crossed the threshold, the great stone door swung up behind them and closed with a *boom* that shook the floor.

"No way back," murmured Sam.

The new chamber was the size of a hall, lit by flaming torches. The lofty walls were covered with painted scenes of people and animals; and gods that were half-animal and half-human – all depicted in the Egyptian style.

Amy walked along the walls, staring up at the pictures.

"I bet Charlie would be able to explain it to us," Sam said.

Without Charlie's brainpower, we might never figure out our next move.

"Do you see any clues?" Sam asked after fruitlessly examining the pictures for several minutes.

"I think some of it is about the journey to the afterlife," Amy began hesitantly. "Wait! This part doesn't look Egyptian."

She was staring at a section of the far

wall. The style of those pictures was quite different, Sam could see that at once. The figures were more realistic, some of them facing out into the room, their poses less stiff, their clothing more medieval than Ancient Egyptian.

"It's Avantian," he breathed, thinking back to similar pictures in Karita's castle.

He felt sudden warmth in his Arcane Band. He raised his arm at exactly the same moment as Amy.

She must be feeling it, too. But what's happening?

A flash burst from both Bands, bathing the wall in golden light.

Sam gazed in astonishment as the

painted figures came alive. There was a dark chamber. A chest. An armoured figure wearing an Arcane Band.

"That's ... *Karita*!" Amy stared up at a young woman with long dark hair and eyes like burning stars. Karita opened the chest. It teemed with Beast eggs of every colour and pattern.

Then a new figure entered the chamber. Tall, sinister – green fire dancing in his palms.

"Malvel," breathed Sam, his heart racing.

The Dark Wizard attacked Karita, but four more armoured figures burst into the room. Two young men and one young woman – led by a tall, broad-shouldered man, bearded, fierce as an eagle, swinging a great shining sword.

"That's Tom, the Master of the Beasts!" gasped Amy as the battle played out silently in front of them. "And the others are Guardians – our grandparents."

Sam nodded; his eyes fixed on the wall. They were seeing something that had happened a long time ago in another world.

Outnumbered, Malvel opened a portal, clutching the chest in both hands. There was a wild flurry of activity. One of the Guardians snatched the chest and fell backwards into the portal. Two others tumbled after him, as did Malvel. The last Guardian leapt through as the edges of the portal wavered and shrank.

The scene changed. Now, three of the young Guardians were in Egypt – in Karnak.

"They have an egg with them," Sam breathed.

The animated figures began to slow down, colours fading, their limbs becoming jerky.

They're turning back into paintings.

The golden glow from the Bands faded – but a disturbing image floated above them.

A gigantic black insect, its head lined with serrated edges, its forelimbs powerful and saw-toothed.

"Th-that's a scarab," exclaimed Amy, backing away.

"It looks freaky, but it's only a picture," Sam said as the light faded away and his Band became cool again.

"Is it?" murmured Amy.

A deep, throbbing growl sounded from above.

Sam glanced up as something big hurtled down at them. He sprang forward, catching Amy around the waist and dragging her out of the path of the plummeting object.

It landed with a crash that shook the chamber.

Dust spiralled up and for a few moments, Sam couldn't make anything out.

Once the dust settled the thing begin to move. It was a greenish black and as

huge as a car with saw-toothed pincers on either side of its great armoured head. Sam choked on a sudden nauseating stench. He remembered that a scarab was a kind of dung beetle – and this one stank in the worst way.

"Nope, you're right. It's real!" he yelled, activating his Arcane Band so that the hook and chain reeled out. "And it's alive!"

"It must be guarding the egg!" Amy was already on her feet, her spiked mace raised in two hands as the monster turned towards her, pincer-legs clacking, sharp as chainsaws. Wuko bounded on to the creature's back, pressing his hands down on the domed armour. Flashes of white energy burst from Wuko's hands, but his beams rebounded off the scarab's back, flinging him across the room with a wail.

The scarab was unharmed.

Spark flew in a tight circle above the creature, spraying its hide with fire. But the red flames rolled off the monster's black shell.

"Keep back!" Sam swung his hook and skimmed it across the floor. His plan was to sweep the monster's legs from under it – maybe tip it on to its back so they could get to its vulnerable underparts.

But before the hook made contact, the scarab curled in on itself, becoming a massive black ball. It rolled rapidly towards Sam, its saw-edged pincers jutting from the sides.

"Watch out!" yelled Amy.

Sam jumped high as the deadly pincers swept under him. He flung the hook again, but it glanced off the armoured ball, jarring his arm.

This is going to be tricky!

At the far end of the chamber, the scarab briefly unrolled, its black eyes staring at them as the pincers champed and clashed.

"It's coming again!" yelled Amy as the scarab folded in on itself and barrelled towards them at horrifying speed.

They leaped aside, Amy giving it a blow as it passed. Her attack knocked it off course, but it seemed that no weapon could penetrate the thick hide. The black sphere bounced off the wall and once more the scarab uncurled and glared at them, hissing furiously.

It can't see when it's rolled up. That could work for us!

"Come on, Stinky!" Sam yelled. "Show us what you got!"

The scarab curled up again and came hurtling at them, pincers scything the air.

Sam jumped over the pincer, but instead of trying to avoid the rolling ball, he twisted in the air and barged into it with his shoulder. It spun off at an angle and crashed into the wall, spraying splinters of stone. The scarab opened and glared at

Sam with fury in its eyes.

It curled up again and flung itself at Sam as Amy raced up.

"I get it," she gasped. "Together this time!"

They jumped over the pincers and hurled themselves at the ball. Amy's mace and Sam's hook struck simultaneously, sending it spinning off at an angle.

It smashed into the wall at high speed. Shards of stonework burst into the air as the wall cracked open.

The scarab uncurled, but it seemed dazed now, its pincers waggling as it struggled to get to its feet.

Sam was about to rush in when Amy grabbed him by the arm.

"No – wait!" She pointed upwards.

Cra-a-a-aack!

The cleft in the wall widened, spilling dust and debris.

The scarab let out a howl of rage. But the sound was lost under a louder, deeper roar as parts of the ceiling began to rain down on to its back.

Brown dust plumed across the chamber, sending Sam and Amy staggering back. Wuko bounded out of the clouds, his eyes wide, and clung to Amy's neck.

"Spark!" called Sam. The little dragon flew to him with a shrill cry.

The rumble and crash of falling masonry died away and the dust-cloud settled. The scarab was half buried in the wreckage.

"Is it dead?" asked Amy.

There was a blue flash and the fallen chunks of stone collapsed in on themselves as the scarab vanished.

"Question asked – question answered," said Sam.

A new, magical light glowed from the crack in the wall.

"This means we've passed the test," said Amy, pointing. "And the egg is through there."

NINE

They clambered over the rubble and squeezed through the glowing crack.

The magical light came from blue crystals set high in the walls of a small chamber. A great oval casket filled the floor, painted in gold and deep blue.

"That's a sarcophagus," breathed Amy, gazing around. The walls were illustrated with tall, stately figures, coloured in deep reds and dusky yellows. Statues stood stiffly in niches.

Amy peered closer. *Are they statues?*

They stood with their arms folded across their chests – swathed in layers of brown, decaying bandages.

"Mummies!" gasped Sam. "I *love* mummies!"

"I don't," Amy said in a low voice. "They're creepy."

She approached the sarcophagus, her senses tingling. The lid was chest-height. The air was electric, and her hearing implants were picking up a gentle humming.

Set in a bowl-shaped depression at the heart of the sarcophagus was an egg.

"Sam – it's here." Amy could feel Wuko trembling with excitement. Even Spark was silent, clinging to Sam's shoulder and staring intently at the egg as he approached.

It was an egg like no other they'd seen.

Amy moved closer, holding her breath.

The surface shimmered with shades of green that moved like oil. The egg seemed to be translucent – Amy almost fancied she could see a shape curled up inside.

"What kind of Beast might it be?" she breathed, mesmerised by the strange way the green oils crawled and slid over the shell.

"Karita will know," said Sam. "We need to get it to her."

Amy leaned over the sarcophagus and took the egg in both hands. It felt cool and smooth under her skin.

She slipped it into her backpack.

Sam grinned at her. "Mission accomplished," he said. "Now to find Charlie and Sali."

"And portal out of here before Illia Raven arrives." Amy added. She looked around the chamber. "But how do we get out?"

The tomb had no obvious exits.

"We can go back," Sam suggested.

"The door to that other chamber closed behind us," Amy said. "I don't think we're going to get it open."

Wuko gazed at her with a wrinkled brow.

"What is it, Wuko?" she asked. He made some chattering noises then leaped off her shoulder. While Amy and Sam stared, Wuko raced around the room, touching the walls, sometimes pressing his ear to them, as though listening for something.

"What's he doing?" asked Sam.

"I'm not sure," Amy admitted.

Suddenly, Wuko gave a whoop and began gesturing wildly at a raised stone in the chamber floor.

Experimentally, Sam stepped on to it. There was a rasp as a section of the wall slid away to reveal rising stone steps.

Amy took out her phone and shone its light upwards. "It's a really long flight. It must go all the way back to the surface," she said. "Wuko! You're the cleverest Beast that ever lived."

Wuko grinned and shrugged as if to say, *It was nothing, really.*

"We're out of here," said Sam.

They climbed, Wuko scrambling in the lead, Amy close behind and Sam at the rear with Spark on his shoulder.

It was a long climb, with darkness closing in behind and steps stretching away for ever above.

"I see daylight," Amy said.

It was a narrow gap, so tight that Amy had

to take off her backpack to edge through. The heat was intense after the long cool of the underground chambers, and the bright light dazzled her for a few moments. Between tall pillars, the dipping sun cast long shadows across a wide courtyard.

Sam followed, screwing his eyes up as the sunlight hit him.

The courtyard was deserted.

"The site must have closed," Amy said. She looked at her phone. "Five bars! I can try calling Charlie – let him know we got the egg."

"If you get through, tell him Illia Raven's on her way," said Sam. "We need to get out of here before—"

Spark sprang suddenly off his shoulder, spiralling upwards, shrieking in alarm.

"Too late!" Sam groaned.

High in the sky, a black dot moved in from the east like a guided missile.

"Spark – come back," yelled Sam. "You're giving us away."

The little dragon swooped down and landed on Sam's outstretched wrist.

The dot swerved in the sky, growing larger as it dived in over the Karnak temple complex.

Amy activated her Arcane Band, feeling the mace appear in her hand. She watched the drone as it drew nearer, her feet braced, her heart pumping, her mouth dry.

The egg was safe in her backpack – and she would fight to the death to protect it.

This drone carried a familiar figure. Her red hair streamed out; her green coat spread around her like leathery wings.

"Did you miss me?" Illia Raven called down in a mocking voice. "Look at you, out in the sun with no sunscreen on – you'll get burnt."

"I don't burn so easy," Sam shouted, whirling his hook and chain.

Amy narrowed her eyes. *What's that she's wearing around her head?*

It was a curious metal headband strung with wires.

Some new weapon Illia's invented. But

what does it do?

"No need to get snarky. I've only popped in for a chat," called Illia, slowly descending until she was hovering just above the ground. "I'm not here to fight."

"How stupid do you think we are?" shouted Amy, raising her mace.

"I haven't decided," Illia replied, smirking. "But I'm thinking ... very, *very* stupid?" Her fingers tapped at her wristband.

Amy heard a whir behind them. She spun around as two drones glided between the temple's pillars. Just like the one that had attacked them in Hyde Park, these had circular frames and were carrying armadillo robots. As they skimmed the ground, the armadillos uncurled and opened fire.

Whiplashes of green electric fire flicked across the courtyard. Amy just managed to dodge the volley. Sam wasn't so lucky – a crackling tongue of energy wrapped around his arm and ripped him off his feet while Spark shrieked and spat fire.

"I've adapted them into energy whips," Illia Raven called.

Wuko leaped at the hissing and flaring lash, but it flicked aside and struck the back of his head, sending him tumbling to the ground with a wail.

Shocked, Amy ran for him, but the other armadillo's electric whip snared her ankle, pulling her feet out from under her.

She hit the ground, pain exploding through her as she kicked to try and get free. The sizzling lash lifted her into the air, upside down, struggling wildly and swinging her mace.

"Too easy," came Illia's derisive voice. "I'll take that egg now, young lady, before it gets broken."

Illia dropped from the drone, her eyes green as poison. Amy swung the mace, but Illia caught her arm, fingers like pincers, nails digging into her flesh.

The pain in her leg from the electric flail was so intense that Amy could hardly think. She stared down into Illia's face, seeing cold vicious contempt in her eyes.

"I win – you lose," Illia hissed. "Are you willing to die to protect the egg?" Her voice came between gritted teeth. "The new Beast will be mine!"

TEN

Charlie was swept along by the water with Sali clinging on to his shirt front. He was disorientated and blinded by rushing bubbles, but there was no pain in his chest; no fear of drowning.

"We need to get out of here, Sali. I'm going to try something," he told his Beast.

He tried to picture the temple complex above.

There must be some water up there that

Sali can send us through.

"OK, open a portal for us, Sali!"

Suddenly, he was moving at a crazy speed, his body spinning like a corkscrew.

He was spat out into a room similar to the one at the museum. Another men's toilet – but this time he'd emerged from a bucket of soapy water standing in a corner.

He eyed the dirty water, relieved that Sali's portals left them dry.

I hope this is the right place.

He ran to the door and peered out at the familiar ruins of Karnak.

"Hmmm – no people, though. The site must be closed." He stepped into the open, gently stroking his Beast's head. "Great job, Sali!"

In the distance, he could hear his cousins' voices and Charlie's stomach tightened. From the sound of it, something bad was going on.

He concentrated on his Arcane Band and the axe slipped into his hand. Sali had tucked herself inside his shirt and was staring out with goggling eyes, her six feet padding nervously at his chest.

Don't worry – I won't let anything happen to you.

The long warm tongue licked his chin and he smiled.

Best Beast in the world.

Charlie darted through a colonnade as he followed the sounds of voices. He rounded a corner to see two of Illia Raven's armadillo drones facing off against his cousins.

Illia? How did she track us down?

He gasped in shock to see writhing streams of green energy pour from the armadillos' blasters. Sam was struggling on the ground, wrapped all around with the energy whiplash while Spark screeched above him, wings beating wildly. Amy was in the air, hanging by one ankle from the other drone's whip – and Illia was underneath her, gripping her arm. Charlie saw the telltale bulge in Amy's backpack.

They found the egg!

Charlie raced for the drone that held Amy. He leaped on to its back, slamming the axe-head against the muzzle of its weapon. The energy lash sprayed out like a Catherine wheel off the face of Charlie's weapon.

Amy fell, landing on Illia and crushing her to the ground.

Charlie grimaced, straining to hold his axe in place as the machine's energy started to feed back into it.

Another moment or two ...

The blaster exploded, throwing Charlie off the creature's back.

"Whoooa!" He scrambled up and jumped as the armadillo's tail swiped at him, scything the air with bone-breaking force.

The robot turned, eyes flashing, jaws opening.

Charlie's axe became a shield as the long metal tongue reeled out, wrapping around the rim and yanking him off his feet. He panicked for a moment, then allowed himself to be dragged towards the stamping machine.

Keep calm. Let it pull you within axe-reach. You can do this.

At the last moment, he switched his shield back into an axe and swung hard. The robot's tongue snapped under the axe's edge. Charlie leaped, coming down

astride the armadillo's neck. He shoved the axe-head between the jaws and heaved back with all his might.

There was a crack. A shower of sparks belched from the gaping mouth. A foul smell filled Charlie's nostrils as the electronics fused and melted in the device's head.

The stumpy legs buckled, and the machine crumpled to the ground.

"Gotcha!" Charlie panted.

He stared across the courtyard to where Illia Raven and Amy were fighting furiously. Illia stabbed with her energy lance and Amy was being driven back, fending off the attack with her mace.

The second armadillo had risen into the air, its electrical whiplash holding Sam down as he struggled and cried out. Spark hovered over the drone, spitting fire – but the shafts of flame bounced off the armour.

Charlie saw a small bundle of fur lying on the ground.

Wuko!

Amy's Beast stirred – he was still alive.

What to do? C'mon, Charlie. Think!

A desperate plan formed. He focused his mind on his Beast.

"Wuko! Spark!" he shouted.

Wuko jumped up, tilting his head toward Charlie, and Spark did much the same.

"Follow me!" Charlie called, breaking

into a run back toward the building with the toilets. When Charlie turned he was pleased to see Wuko and Sali bounding after him and Spark flying close to his shoulder.

I hope they'll understand what I need.

"Sali – where's the main water pipe?" he asked once they were all inside.

Sali skittered around the floor, her head low. She stopped under one of the sinks and looked up at him. "Good girl!" He beckoned and she jumped into his arms.

"Spark, we have to break through the floor."

Spark hovered, raining fire down on to the tiles. They smoked, melted and burst apart as a fierce jet of water gushed up, splashing off the ceiling.

"Good job! Wuko – can you take out those windows?" Frosted-glass windows ran along the front wall. Wuko bounded up, white energy pouring from his hands. The windows exploded outwards.

Fighting the deluge of water, Charlie hacked at the broken pipe, jamming his axe-head under it and levering upwards so the powerful jet gushed out through the broken windows. He was aiming for the remaining armadillo drone.

Sali leaped on to the windowsill, raising a splayed hand to gesture to the right.

Charlie hammered at the pipe to shift

the jet of water and Sali bounced excitedly on the windowsill.

Bingo!

Charlie raced to the door. He saw the powerful burst of water flood off the armadillo's armour. The force of it knocked it sideways. Charlie could hear its insides grating together as black smoke billowed from the seams in its armour.

The water has short-circuited it!

A moment later, the electrical whiplash died and Sam was free.

Sam picked himself up. "Way to go, Charlie!" he gasped.

"It was a team effort!" Charlie shouted back.

Charlie and Sam both ran towards Amy and Illia Raven. Amy had her back to a wall, swinging her mace as Illia stabbed with her lance.

Amy dodged the blow by diving forwards, barging between Illia's leg and tipping the woman over. But Illia seized the moment to snatch at Amy's backpack and ripped it from her shoulders.

"The egg is mine!" Illia screamed triumphantly.

She touched her wrist-control and her drone swooped down to pick her up. She was lifted into the air a moment before Sam and Charlie could get to her.

She hung above them, her face split by a

grin, and brandished the backpack as Amy got to her feet.

"One move and I smash the egg," Illia called down.

Sam let his hook and chain drop. The three cousins stared up helplessly as the drone carried Illia to the top of the wall.

Illia drew the Beast egg from the backpack.

"While there's breath in our lungs, we'll fight you," Amy shouted.

"Yes, dear, very nice," Illia mocked. "But I know something you don't." She lifted her hand to the curious circlet around her forehead. "Anyone want to guess what this is?"

"A fairy tiara made from wire coat hangers?" Sam taunted.

A spasm of anger crossed Illia's face. "It's my Energy Crown."

"Wow! Talk about delusions of grandeur!" laughed Amy. "So, you're a queen now, are you?"

"I'll be empress of the entire world soon enough," Illia shouted. "I know how to hatch Beast eggs using science." She held the green egg up high, gazing at it. "Such a pretty thing."

The spikes on her crown began to spark. Threads of green lightning licked over the egg.

Charlie's stomach tightened in alarm.

She can't do this! Only a Guardian can hatch an egg!

A thin crack ran across the shell.

"All hail the queen!" cried Illia and she began to laugh maniacally. "Empress of all the Beasts!"

The three cousins watched in alarm as the crack widened.

The egg was hatching.

ELEVEN

How is this possible? Sam stared in dismay at the splitting egg. *Illia's not a Guardian!*

Illia Raven cupped the egg, her face bathed in an eerie green glow as the shell broke open.

Green fog snaked out of the egg. A dark shape writhed inside.

"Remember what Karita told us about Beasts?" Charlie murmured.

Amy nodded. "They can be evil if the

wrong person hatches them."

Spark settled on to Sam's shoulder. Wuko was on the ground, clinging to Amy's leg. Sali was hanging from Charlie's shirt-front. All three creatures were absolutely silent, staring up the hatching Beast.

The green haze faded. Sam gave a gasp, his blood chilling in his veins as he stared up in horror at the apparition in Illia Raven's hands. It stretched out gaunt wings, lifting itself on spindly legs and letting out a terrible shriek.

"Oh, no!" Amy groaned, flinging her hands over her face.

The Beast was in the hideous shape of a skeletal bird, its bony, spreading wings hung with withered feathers, its chest a cave of curling ribs. Green fire ran over its hollow body and along the ragged feathers of its tail. A crest of emerald flame rose from its skull and its eye-sockets burned with green sorcery.

"It's a phoenix!" cried Illia. "Isn't he *beautiful*?" Her eyes reflected the green flames. "His name is Pox."

The creature rose into the air, its wings flapping slowly, trailing streams of green fire. It circled Illia, screaming in a piercing voice that made Sam feel sick. On his shoulder, Spark shivered. Wuko was moaning softly in Amy's arms.

They're terrified of it.

The ghastly bird dropped down and landed on Illia's shoulders, bony talons gripping hard. Illia winced as the Beast breathed green fire into her face. She rocked back, gasping and choking.

That's so gross.

Illia balanced herself, panting hard, a sickly pallor distorting her face.

"We have to destroy that crown," muttered Charlie. "Before things go too far."

"How much further can they go?" breathed Sam.

"I think this is just the start," Amy groaned. "With that crown, she can hatch any egg and the Beast will be bonded to her. She could have an army of Beasts!"

As they stared up, Illia stepped off the wall, the Beast's claws gripping her shoulders. Pox spread his wings over her as she descended, both of them enveloped in flickering green fire.

"Let's do this!" said Sam, swinging his chain.

Everyone acted at once. Spark shot into the air, spitting fire. Wuko bounded on to Amy's head, his hands open, pouring out white energy. Amy had her mace ready; Charlie held his axe in both hands.

Sam flicked his wrist and the chain whirled around Illia's legs.

I'll drag her down here ... She can't beat

all six of us.

But hoops of green fire pulsed down from Pox's wings towards Sam, sending him staggering back.

Amy swung her mace, but was driven to her knees by the green fire. Charlie pulled her away as the sickly flames gnawed into the ground. Wuko's energy beams skittered across Pox's wings without causing damage.

"See how mighty we are!" Illia crowed at the Guardians.

But then something strange happened.

Pox unhooked his talons from Illia and she dropped to the ground. The skeletal Beast rained green flames on his mistress, engulfing her body in infernal fire. She screamed in agony, her back twisted, her entire body shuddering.

Something's wrong!

Sam closed in on Illia as she stumbled and fell on to one knee.

"Was that tiara *meant* to turn you into a monster?" Sam called. "Because I think that's what's happening."

Illia writhed and moaned as the green fires licked over her.

"Quick, Illia! There'll be nothing left of you," shouted Charlie. "That crown's not working right and the Beast is taking you over."

"Take the crown off," cried Amy.

"We'll smash it!"

Illia became still.

They waited, unsure of what was happening. Pox beat his shrivelled wings into the air and behind them, the water poured noisily on to the flagstones from the ruptured pipe. Pools spread across the courtyard.

Illia finally raised her head. Green veins pulsed under her skin and there was a deadly light in her eyes.

A venomous smile slashed across her face. "Too late," she growled. Her voice was deeper and seemed to echo as if spoken from a terrible depth. "Far too late."

Is that her? She sounds different.

Illia got to her feet, cupping her hands, green fire dancing in her palms.

"This Beast power is the most intense of all." Her eyes widened as she stared at the three Guardians. "I can see all the dead of the world. I can *command* them."

She spread her arms, curling her fingers, immersed in green fire.

"Awake, children of darkness!" she cried. "Rise from your graves! Aid me in my conquest!"

"What's she doing?" gasped Sam, his skin crawling.

"Something terrible," said Amy.

The ground cracked beneath their feet, great rumbling fissures ripping across the courtyard. A foul air flowed up, as though all the coffins in the world had been thrown open.

Sam's head filled with a nauseating stench.

"Something's coming," said Charlie, his voice trembling.

Scrabbling sounds echoed from the deep clefts. A gnarled hand snatched at the ground. Then another. And another. Dust-dry creatures rose out of the earth, swathed in rotting bandages. Their faces were just wasted skin over raw bones, and their hollow eyes seethed with green fire.

It's the mummies from the tomb. She's brought them back to life!

"I like mummies, but still, not cool, Illia!" shouted Sam, swinging his hook and chain as the first of the mummies moved towards them.

"I have only just begun," Illia roared, rising on a pillar of swirling green flame. She lifted her arms, her fingers pouring fire. "I shall open every grave in Egypt," she howled. "I shall raise an army from their graves to sweep across entire continents." She gave a crazed laugh. "I am Empress of the Dead and all the world shall bow before me!"

TWELVE

Amy's heart broke as she watched Illia Raven pour her green fire across the sky.

Charlie said there's a huge necropolis on the other side of the Nile – she's going to bring all those dead people back to life.

A bony hand grabbed her arm, snapping her out of her despair. The mummy loomed over her, its face a mask of rotting skin, its eyes livid with green flame. It leaned in, open-mouthed, brown teeth straining to tear at her throat.

She swung her mace at the skull, and it exploded into fragments. But the creature's hand still clung to her, the fingers biting into her flesh. She struck at the mummy's arm, the barbed end of her mace tearing through decayed bandages, ripping into dry skin and smashing bones.

The body crumbled, but still the fingers clawed her arm. Disgusted and horrified, she prised the fingers loose one by one and the hand fell away. It twitched on the ground.

"Horrible!" She pounded the hand to powder, her heart thundering, her stomach a knot of stone under her ribs.

The battle raged all around her. Hands caught her from behind. She steeled herself to fight to the death. There was a *swish*; ripping and slashing noises. She spun around. Sam's hook and chain had taken the heads off two mummies. Their bodies staggered until he caught them by the knees with the back-swing and sent them tumbling.

"They don't stop!" Sam gasped, his face ashen. "You have to smash them to pieces!"

"I know!" Amy swung her mace at the headless monsters. Arms and legs flew apart as she beat them to the ground.

A little way off, Charlie stood with his back to a wall, holding off four mummies with his axe while Wuko blasted them with beams of white energy.

But the beams were weakening – and Amy could sense her Beast's unease. He needed fresh energy from some outside source. But the mummy army was dead – there was no energy to draw on.

Amy's attention was drawn upwards by shrieking and hissing noises and the furious flapping of wings. High in the green-hued sky, Pox and Spark were locked in a vicious and deadly battle. As Amy watched, the phoenix's green fire overwhelmed the orange flames from Spark. The little dragon was hurled backwards, her wings churning the air.

The water from the broken pipe flooded the courtyard. Sali leaped from puddle to puddle, flinging herself at the mummies to knock them back, then diving again to emerge instantly somewhere else.

"I don't know how we're going to survive this," Sam said.

"It's the crown," Amy gasped, wiping mummy dust off her face. "It connects Illia with Pox – it's her power source. Break it and we have a chance."

Maniacal laughter rang through the courtyard. Illia Raven stood on her pillar of green fire, her face contorted with evil triumph and her whole body sheathed in flame.

More mummies lumbered in from all sides, jaws champing, hooked fingers clawing.

"Back to back!" Sam cried.

Comforted by the feel of Sam's back against hers, Amy held off the onslaught with every bit of strength and skill. Her mace almost had a life of its own as she swung and parried and struck out at her enemies – her Arcane Band glowing as its ancient power poured through her veins.

"Do not kill them." It was Illia Raven's voice – rasping, inhuman – calling across the courtyard. "I want them to witness the new world that I will create."

"You realise that's not even *her* any

more?" gasped Sam.

"Or if it is her, she's gone insane!" panted Amy.

"And she was pretty crazy to begin with!" Sam agreed.

Amy didn't respond: she needed all her focus, all her energy to keep fighting. Hideous faces lunged at her; dry lips drawn back over gnashing teeth. Bony fingers clawed. And for every mummy she smashed, another took its place.

It's impossible. We can't beat a whole army.

From the corner of her eye, she saw the mummies bring Charlie down. His axe carved the air for a few more moments, sending heads and limbs flying. And then it was over. The mummies lifted him high, spreadeagled between a dozen hands.

Where are you, Wuko?

She saw her Beast. He had been thrust into the ribcage of one of the mummies, all his energies depleted, his dull eyes staring through the bars of the ribs, too weak to escape.

A rope of green fire spat from Illia's hand to coil around Sam's chain, jerking him from his feet and lifting him into the air. Illia swept her arm sideways and Sam was dashed against a wall.

With a cry of pain, he crashed to the ground. He made no move as the mummies closed in on him.

"Surrender and I will spare you!" Illia croaked, staring down at Amy.

"Never!"

Gritting her teeth, Amy fought on, her body tingling with energy, the power of the Arcane Band racing through her veins. She leaped high, tumbling through the air, kicking out as she somersaulted over the repulsive heads of the mummies. She struck out with her mace, knocking skulls from shoulders, breaking arms and pulverising bodies.

Illia's fiery whip pursued her, always half a beat behind her cartwheeling legs and ducking head. Amy's muscles screamed for relief, her mouth and nose clogged with mummy dust. But then her foot clipped the shoulder of a mummy, throwing her off-balance. She lost momentum, windmilling her arms as she landed heavily and staggered a few paces on leaden feet. She couldn't find her centre of gravity. With a cry, she tripped over a fallen mummy and sprawled on her back, gasping for breath.

A host of hands reached for her. Struggling and crying out, she was dragged upright. Illia's rope wound around her chest, burning her, pinning her arms to her sides.

Still straining to get free, Amy watched helplessly as Illia glided down towards her.

She stood for a moment, staring into

Amy's eyes.

"Perhaps I do not need to keep you all alive," she spat. "*Your* death will serve as a warning to the others." The green fire crawled up Amy's body and clenched tight around her throat. She gasped, pain searing through her body.

On the edge of her vision, she saw Spark tumbling through the air, engulfed in Pox's fires. But there was something else.

Sali dived into a puddle on the far side of the courtyard – and a moment later she launched herself from another puddle, immediately behind Illia Raven.

There was something else with her. Something huge and dark, with heavy scales and long snapping jaws and a great, thick writhing tail.

A crocodile!

The massive creature jetted up from the puddle, hung in the air for a moment, then came crashing down on top of Illia with all its weight and bulk.

The villain was smashed to the ground, howling in shock and pain.

Her mummies' grips on Amy loosened. She tore herself free from them and lunged forwards, snatching the energy crown off Illia's head.

She flung it to the ground and brought her mace crashing down. With a flash and an electric crackle, the crown broke into a

thousand fragments.

The green fires died and a low groaning came from the mummies. Before Amy could react, they burst into clouds of dust that drifted and settled like ash.

A grinding noise echoed through the courtyard as the fissures in the ground closed.

The crocodile writhed, its short legs scrabbling as it heaved its great body off the fallen woman. Sali blinked at Illia Raven, then at Amy, then peered into a pool of water that lay under the crocodile's belly – and in an instant, the massive creature fell through it and was gone.

Back to the Nile, thought Amy, still

dazed. *The poor thing must have found that very confusing.*

She stooped over Illia and turned her on to her back, hoping she wasn't dead. Her power was gone. She was no longer a threat. Sali could teleport them all back to Karita's castle – and Karita could decide what to do with Illia.

"Are you OK?" Amy said, shaking the woman's shoulder.

Illia Raven's eyes opened blearily.

"My crown ..."

"Broken," said Amy.

"You'll pay for that." Illia sat up weakly, gasping for breath.

Amy shook her head. "Give up, Illia," she

said. "You lost."

"Watch out, Amy!" Charlie shouted. Amy looked up in time to see Pox diving for her. His talons were just centimetres from her face when Sam's hook wound around its body. The Beast only had time to let out a shrill yip as Sam hurled it to the ground.

Wuko and Spark wasted no time in joining the attack. Flames struck the shrieking phoenix as energy bolts sent his bones crackling with energy. Charlie launched himself at the twisted Beast with his axe and Amy hammered at his wings with her mace.

Pox struggled and twitched with smouldering, foul green flames. The phoenix screeched and his sickly light grew brighter and brighter.

"He's going to blow!" Sam cried.

A great flare of green light forced Amy to look away.

When she turned back, Pox was nothing but bones.

"Did we beat him?" Charlie asked, standing alongside Amy.

"I don't know," Amy said breathlessly. "Sam, don't get too close!"

Sam had hurried forward to crane over the pile of bones.

"Guys, something's weird here," he said.

A green light flared across his face. Amy saw a spike of emerald flame burst from the bones. "Sam! Get back!"

Sam scampered backwards as the pile of bones ignited. A moment later there was an otherworldly shriek and Pox launched himself from the flames.

"He's been reborn!" Charlie shouted.

"Pox is a phoenix," Amy said in wonder and horror. "Maybe he can't be killed."

The Guardians threw themselves to the ground as Pox swooped down like a thunderbolt.

The phoenix's claws hooked into Illia's shoulders and in a flurry of flame-rimmed wings, he rose again, carrying her up into the sky.

Amy leaped up, but Illia was already out

of reach. The limp woman stared down with a look of pure hatred as the hideous Beast carried her over the walls. They fled high into the sky, dwindling to a dot then vanishing from sight.

Charlie and Sam ran up.

"She got away," Amy groaned.

"But you smashed her crown and the mummies are all gone," Sam pointed out. "That's something."

"And all thanks to Sali," cried Charlie, grinning from ear to ear. "Where is she?"

Wuko bounded towards Amy, leaped up and clung around her neck. She smiled at the way the little Beast fizzed with energy.

With a shrill cry, Spark soared on to

Sam's head and settled with her claws clinging gently to his hair.

Then a spurt of water burst from the severed pipe. Sali appeared in mid-air, all six legs waving.

"Way to go, girl!" Charlie caught his Beast in his arms.

Amy couldn't help laughing as a long thin tongue came out and licked all over Charlie's face.

The Guardians were reunited with their Beasts and for the time being Illia Raven was no longer a threat to the world.

Not a bad day's work!

THIRTEEN

Charlie and Sali were first out of the fountain. Charlie staggered, finding his balance with difficulty and almost face-planting in the gravel. Sam was next, landing neatly with Spark on his shoulder, and followed by Amy, sure-footed, holding Wuko in her arms.

Karita and Varla were waiting for them.

They told Karita everything, often talking over one another, and with Sam acting out especially exciting parts, while Charlie added corrections here and there.

"I feel bad about the mess we made of the temple," Charlie admitted.

"Do not reproach yourselves," Karita said. "I'll make an anonymous donation to cover the repairs."

"You should have seen Amy whack Illia's headgear!" exclaimed Sam. "She won't be using that again."

"And yet what science makes once, it can make again," Karita said. "And it was this crown that allowed her to hatch the Beast egg?"

Amy nodded. "Right in front of us."

Karita shook her head, frowning deeply.

"It should not be possible," she muttered.

"And just when we thought she was toast, that gruesome undead-bird thing swooped in and carried her off," said Sam. "I hate when that happens."

"That's twice she's got away," said Charlie. "You can bet she's off somewhere, licking her wounds and plotting her big comeback."

Karita nodded gravely. "That is certain," she said. "From all you say, Illia Raven has appetites for conquest that rival those of Malvel himself. Further, she appears to have a strange Beast of incredible power."

"And don't forget, that thing won't stay dead," Sam added.

"Did we fail, Karita?" asked Amy. "Letting her escape again?"

Karita's eyes burned with pride. "No, indeed, Guardians," she said. "You and your Beasts did very well." She gazed into the sky, as though her thoughts were suddenly far, far away.

"But now that Illia Raven has Pox, she'll be more dangerous than ever. I am disturbed, too, by what you said that she seemed to change while bonded to this skeletal phoenix. It could be the threat they pose is even worse than we know." She looked from Charlie to Amy to Sam, her hand gently stroking Varla's velvety head. "We may need help if we are to defeat her and Pox once and for all."

"What kind of help?" asked Charlie.

Karita's dark eyes smouldered. "Help from Avantia!" she said.

THE END

If you enjoyed this book, don't miss the
new series of

Read on for a sneak peek at
ELECTRO THE STORM BIRD . . .

1

A DAY LONG AWAITED

Tom sat straight-backed on the raised dais near the king and queen, his stomach churning with nerves as he gazed over the crowded courtyard. The jewelled outfits and dress armour of the assembled guests shone in the morning sun, dazzling him. A fresh breeze made the palace flags ripple and snap overhead, and colourful bunting fluttered all along the courtyard walls.

"I'm not used to all this attention," Tom muttered to Elenna, who sat close by his side. Most of the court and palace guard had assembled to watch him receive his powers back. Even his aunt and uncle had come all the way from Errinel. When he caught Aunt Maria's eye, she waved, her face glowing with pride.

"You've earned it," Elenna whispered. "If we hadn't got the Circle of Wizards' artefacts back from the Locksmith, goodness knows what trouble we'd be facing now. Restoring your powers is the least they could do."

Tom had to agree she was right. The Circle's stolen items had accidentally released a fiery Beast called Scalamanx that he'd had to defeat.

"Will the magic lot ever turn up?" grumbled Captain Harkman, from his station just behind them. "It is unforgivable to keep the king and queen waiting like this."

A sudden flash of white light blinded Tom, and startled yelps and gasps ran through the crowd. When Tom's vision cleared, he saw two figures in flowing purple gowns edged with gold, standing on the dais before Hugo and

Aroha – Sorella, the head of the Circle, and a young wizard, Stefan. Beside them, two burly men in armour carried a hefty-looking chest. The king and queen smiled welcomingly, but Sorella and Stefan turned away to face the crowd without giving them so much as a nod.

"Insolence!" Harkman growled.

Sorella lifted a hand, waiting for silence. Then she spoke in a solemn voice: "After a long and valiant struggle, setting aside all personal comforts for the good of Avantia, this day has finally come," she said. "Few have sacrificed so much. Few have striven with such courage in the face of adversity." Sorella paused to gather her audience, and Elenna nudged Tom.

Read ELECTRO THE STORM BIRD
to find out what happens …